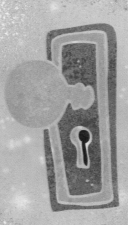

For Aidan and Lara.
My inspiration.
Loved always.

x

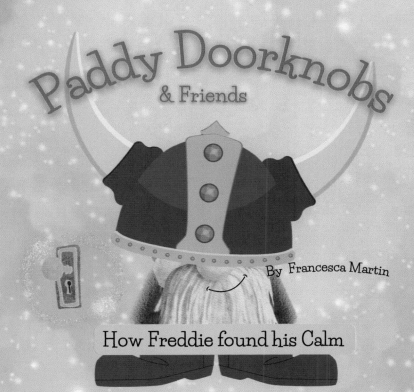

Paddy Doorknobs
& Friends

By Francesca Martin

How Freddie found his Calm

Have YOU ever felt a strange tingle, a
breeze through the back of your hair?

You reach right around to see what it is,
and find that nothing is there?

This happened to Freddie, a regular thing,
just about every day.
He would turn around quickly, only to
find, it had quietly gone away.

One day in school , Freddie tried hard to listen, he could hear the teacher explaining.

Everyone seemed to understand what she said, so there was no use in complaining.

He copied the numbers she wrote on the board, and continued to stare at the chart.

He did not understand, and was getting quite cross, he definitely didn't feel smart.

That's when he felt it, right there again, a whisper of breeze on his skin.

His head whipped round fast, to take a good look, certain that he saw wings.

Mrs Peters had given them homework to do,
Freddie knew he would have to try.

But it was difficult sums from school that day, and
he felt tears start to fall from his eyes.

Slumped on his bed feeling cross and alone,
staring angrily down at his book,

He felt that whistle of gentle wind, but this time,
it came with a THUD!

He leapt up so quickly, right off his bed, his workbook slid onto the floor.

Then crept over slowly, and ever so carefully, quietly to the door.

First, he noticed the shiny brass doorknob, it had never looked sparkly before.

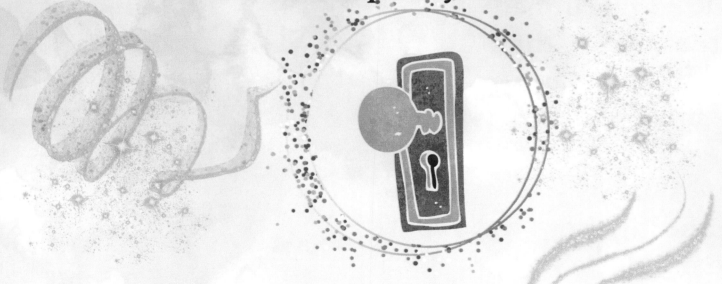

But wide eyed in shock, he stared in surprise, at who was there at the door.

Blinking his eyes,
Freddie rubbed
them hard, then
blinked, and
blinked again.

What he saw
standing there was
an odd little fellow
who gave him a
wide friendly grin.

"Hello...Wh..who are you?" Freddie struggled to mutter, and continued to blink his shocked eyes.

He was left open mouthed when the creature sat down and gently, calmly replied.

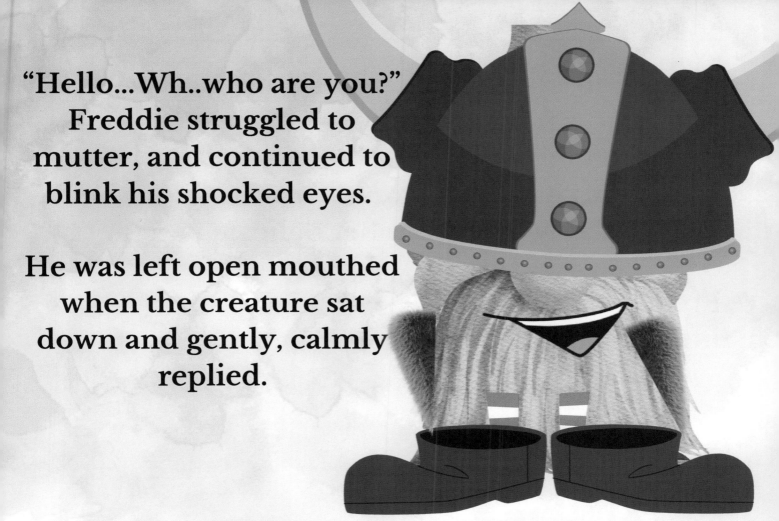

"My name is Paddy Doorknobs I have seen that you're cross, and I've come to help you with that".

"You have been struggling lately with some of your work, and especially with your maths"

"My best friend's a fairy, I know that you've noticed a few little odd and strange things."

"Those tingles you felt on the back of your neck, are the breeze from her delicate wings"

Freddie was scared, a little bit frightened, he was not too afraid to admit that.

But he was starting to warm to this friendly small fellow who was roughly the size of a cat.

He absorbed every detail, for when he could give,
his best friend Charlotte the facts.

The stripy short legs, the long scraggy beard and the
oversized Viking horned hat.

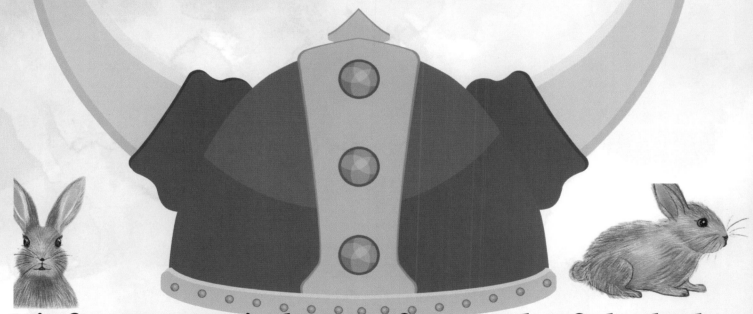

His forest green jacket was furry and soft, looked
like a fluffy old bunny,

With thousands of pockets, which jingled and
clinked as they moved with his round little tummy.

Then Paddy stood up, and Freddie soon noticed, the enormous size of his feet.

He wondered, right then, how on earth he would manage to walk a straight line down the street.

Finally Freddie, found his lost voice, and slowly began to speak

"Hi Paddy Doorknobs, it's great to meet you", in a sound that came out like a squeak.

"The trouble with things we think are hard work" said Paddy, his voice soft and low.

"Is the more that we look, the more jumbled it seems, but try this, and lets see how we go."

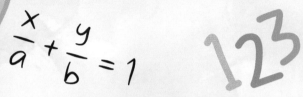

$$\frac{x}{a} + \frac{y}{b} = 1$$

"I see you've been trying ever so hard, with all sorts of school work, like maths."

"Yet try as you might, you can't get it right, I will help you get on the right path."

Paddy sat down and crossed his short legs;
his back tall and straight like a tree.

He motioned to Freddie to follow his lead,
softly resting his hands on his knees.

Freddie was very
confused at this point
and asked Paddy what
he should do.

"If you feel like you're
struggling getting angry
or cross, here's a great
little rhyme you can
use."

"Breathe in through your nose, count to three in your head, hold it in, slowly counting to four."

"Let it out through your mouth whilst counting to five, then try to repeat it once more."

1 2 3 4 5

"That's easy, thought Freddie, and what's more it's great fun, and with Paddy he chanted the rhyme.

When they came to the end, they did it again, and repeated it over five times.

"So how are you feeling Freddie my friend?" Paddy looked at the boy with a smile.

"I feel happy and calm" Freddie said with a grin "Much better than I've felt for a while."

"How does it work?" Freddie wanted to know,
"How can breathing just make you feel good?"

"Its magic" said Paddy, as he heaved himself up
"It helps you to feel as you should. "

Freddie picked up his maths book and started
to work, he was relaxed and calmer than ever.

"I've done it!" he squealed, in utter delight,
"I feel like I really am clever".

"You've really done well, I'm proud of you Freddie, always use that rhyme when it's tough."

Paddy outstretched his arms, Freddie knelt for a hug, he couldn't thank his new friend enough.

Then Freddie felt it again, that familiar breeze, right on the back of his hair.

This time he turned, and to his surprise, saw a flutter of wings on the air.

"It's a fairy!" he cried, not believing his eyes, and watched as she flickered and flew.

"Don't worry" chuckled Paddy "She's my very best friend, may I introduce the lovely LuLu"

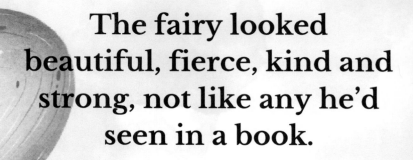

The fairy looked beautiful, fierce, kind and strong, not like any he'd seen in a book.

With ebony hair and sparkly blue eyes, she fixed Freddie a curious look.

Suddenly, gently, she broke into a smile, glitter shimmered around her like rain.

"I'm LuLu" she said, in a warm friendly voice, "I'll help Paddy to get home again"

"We live in a cottage, just a few thoughts away" said Paddy, and slowly arose.

"With LuLu's great magic, we'll be back in no time, to a place most humans don't know."

"We travel through doorknobs and walls of all homes, that is how I got my strange name."

"With a rhyme or two here, and magic dust there, we vanish right through your doorframe."

LuLu flew right to Freddie, whispered soft in his ear, and she gently touched his warm cheek.

"Paddy struggles sometimes, with moving around, he needs help or trips over his feet.

"It's now time to go" Lu-Lu took Paddys hand, and slowly they walked to the door.

With tears in his eyes, Freddie said his goodbye, he hoped he would see them both more.

With a blink of an eye, Freddie watched them leap up, and land on the doorknob with ease.

They vanished from sight in a cloud of pink smoke and Freddie let out a huge sneeze.

In school the next day, Freddie remembered the words, his magic friend Paddy had said.

When he felt a bit cross, confused or just sad, the rhyme would come into his head.

"You think that we're magic, and of course you'd be right, we help children when they feel down."

"But the power is you, you're pure magic yourself, so remember that next time you frown"

"When you're feeling cross and you can't get things right, just always remember the rhyme."

"Say it out loud and breathe in and out, you'll feel better in simply no time."

"Breathe in through your nose, count to three in your head, hold it in, slowly counting to four.

Let it out through your mouth whilst counting to five, then try to repeat it once more"

So, if you are struggling, feel like nobody's listening, just say this rhyme out loudly too.

Maybe Paddy will visit, and LuLu right with him, but really the magic is ..

YOU!

Keep your eyes peeled for more
Paddy Doorknobs & friends
adventures coming soon.....

Printed in Great Britain
by Amazon

87877135R10018